SUPERHERO . . . OR SUPER THIEF?

Don't miss these other nail-biting **MAXimum Boy** adventures:

THE HIJACKING OF MANHATTAN
THE DAY EVERYTHING TASTED LIKE BROCCOLI

MAXimum Boy

starring in
SUPERHERO . . . OR
SUPER THIEF?

BY DAN GREENBURG
ILLUSTRATIONS BY GREG SWEARINGEN

A Little Apple Paperback

SCHOLASTIC INC.
New York   Toronto   London   Auckland   Sydney
Mexico City   New Delhi   Hong Kong   Buenos Aires

No part of this publication may be reproduced in whole or in part, or stored in a retrieval system, or transmitted in any form or by any means, electronic, mechanical, photocopying, recording, or otherwise, without written permission of the publisher. For information regarding permission, write to Scholastic Inc., Attention: Permissions Department, 555 Broadway, New York, NY 10012.

ISBN 0-439-21946-9

Text copyright © 2001 by Dan Greenburg.
Illustrations copyright © 2001 by Scholastic Inc.

All rights reserved. Published by Scholastic Inc.

SCHOLASTIC, LITTLE APPLE PAPERBACKS, and associated logos are trademarks and/or registered trademarks of Scholastic Inc.

12 11 10 9 8 7 6 5 4 3 2 1   1 2 3 4 5 6/0

Printed in the U.S.A.
First Scholastic printing, August 2001

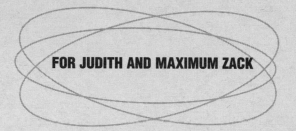

FOR JUDITH AND MAXIMUM ZACK

CHAPTER 1

Usually I don't fly to school in the morning. Usually I walk.

This particular morning I forgot to set my alarm and I overslept. My mom came into my room at eight twenty-five.

"Max!" she said. "You're not up yet? It's eight twenty-five! School starts in five minutes!"

"Uh-oh," I said. "OK. Don't worry, Mom. I'll just fly there."

"You're not going to have breakfast?"

"I don't have *time* for breakfast," I said.

I jumped out of bed and started dressing. First I put on my Maximum Boy uniform, then my regular clothes on top. Dad came into my room.

"You're not going to take a shower?" he asked.

"Dad, there isn't *time*. I have to be at school in five minutes."

"Well, you're not going to school unless you shower and eat, and that's that."

I sighed a really big sigh. My parents are great, but they can sure be a pain about things like showering and eating breakfast.

"OK OK OK," I said. I peeled off my clothes and sprinted for the bathroom in my

Maximum Boy uniform. "Mom, please set me up for a speed breakfast, and make sure the bathroom is clear."

"The bathroom is *not* clear, Max," Mom called after me. "Tiffany is — "

My teenage sister, Tiffany, was brushing her teeth when I got into the bathroom.

"Hey!" she said. "This room is *occupied*, do you *mind*?"

"Sorry, Tiff, but I'm in kind of a hurry. Just close your eyes and I'll be out of here before you know it."

I went into Maximum speed. In half a second I'd whipped off my uniform and jumped into the shower. In another second I'd turned on the hot water, gotten wet, lathered up, rinsed off, grabbed a towel, dried off, jumped back into my uniform, and raced out of the bathroom.

"Mom!" yelled Tiffany. "Max wants to take a shower, but I was in here *first*!"

"Relax, Tiff!" I shouted. "I already *took* my shower. I'm eating breakfast now."

Mom had set me up for a speed breakfast — a bowl of Cheerios, a glass of milk, a glass of orange juice, and a handful of vitamins. I gulped the juice and milk in one second each. I inhaled the vitamins along with the Cheerios. That took two seconds more.

"Don't gulp your food, Max," said my mom.

"Mom, gulping my food is the only way I can do this," I said. "You know that."

"I know, I know," she said.

I looked at my watch. It was now eight twenty-eight. I yelled good-bye and raced out of the apartment.

In case you're wondering how I could

shower, dress, and eat so fast, I better explain.

My name is Max Silver. I live on the north side of Chicago, next to Lake Michigan, with my mom, my dad, and my stupid teenage sister, Tiffany. I'm eleven years old. I have braces, glasses, and superpowers. The superpowers were kind of an accident. I accidentally touched some glowing blue rocks at the Air and Space Museum that had come from outer space.

Right after that I found I could do things most eleven-year-old boys can't. Like lift freight trains. And fly faster than the space shuttle. And burp the alphabet. (Actually, I do know one other kid who can burp the alphabet, but I don't think she can lift freight trains or fly.) When I don't use my superpowers, I'm the second-worst athlete in my grade. But if I use my superpowers I'll blow my cover. And if I did that, my family would be in danger. You'd think I could use just a *little* of my superpowers and just be a *little* stronger and faster than the other kids, but that's not how superpowers work. With superpowers it's all or nothing. I really hate that.

I do have a few weaknesses. Milk products and sweet potatoes give me a bad upset stomach. Ragweed makes me sneeze my head off. And math. It's not just that I'm no good at math, it's that even seeing or *hearing* a math problem makes me weak and dizzy. I'm the only kid in the sixth grade with a doctor's excuse to get out of math. Superman had the same problem with kryptonite.

The President of the United States calls

me all the time to do things that only a superhero could do. Like the time an evil scientist named Dr. Zirkon hijacked the island of Manhattan and towed it out to sea. I rescued Manhattan and towed it back to New York Harbor. Or the time a supervillain named the Tastemaker made everything in the whole country taste like broccoli. I solved that one, too.

Anyway, here I was, flying to school because I overslept. It was now eight twenty-nine. One minute to go before I was late. If you're late in my homeroom, you get detention. You have to stay after school and write compositions about the value of not being late. I was flying at an altitude of about a thousand feet. I looked down. Traffic wasn't moving at all. This was the beginning of morning rush hour, but traffic was completely stopped. There was something funny about this, but I didn't have time to figure out what.

I swooped down and landed on the ground. I changed into my street clothes in one second. I raced into school and down the hallway and into my homeroom. At exactly eight-thirty I slid into my seat.

It was strangely quiet in the classroom. I looked at my teacher, Mrs. Mulvahill. She sat behind her desk, staring straight at me. Why was she staring at me? Was I late? I looked at my watch. It said eight-thirty. I wasn't late. So why was she staring at me?

"It's exactly eight-thirty, Mrs. Mulvahill," I said. "I am not late."

She didn't answer. She didn't move a muscle. She looked like she was frozen stiff. I looked at the kids on all sides of me. They weren't moving, either. A boy named Ben was about to throw a crumpled ball of paper. His hand was frozen in the air. A girl named Jennifer in the row next to me was frozen, painting her fingernail black. A boy on the other side of me named Sherman was frozen, picking his nose. His finger was all the way up his nostril.

And then suddenly I blacked out. I don't know how long I was unconscious. When I woke up, everybody else was still frozen.

Why had everyone else blacked out before me? Why did I wake up while they were still frozen? Maybe it had something to do with my superpowers.

I got up and walked to Mrs. Mulvahill's desk.

"Mrs. Mulvahill?" I whispered.

She didn't answer. She was still frozen.

Oh, no, I thought. She's dead! My teacher and everybody in my homeroom is dead! How did this happen? Was it a neutron bomb? Was it a death ray from a UFO?

I panicked. I ran out of the classroom. In the hallway was a kid named Sheldon from the fifth grade. His locker was open and he was reaching inside it, taking out a book. Usually, I don't talk to kids in the fifth grade.

"Sheldon!" I called. "Get out of the school! Weird forces have attacked Mrs. Mulvahill's homeroom!"

Sheldon didn't move. I walked closer to him. He was frozen stiff.

I ran outside to the street. Nothing was moving. Cars were stopped in all directions. People walking in the street were frozen stiff, some with one foot in the air. A traffic cop on the corner was frozen with his hand in the air, directing traffic. A miniature schnauzer was standing next to a tree, his hind leg frozen while peeing.

Had the whole city stopped? How far had this thing spread? Had it spread back as far as my home? To my family? I changed into my Maximum Boy uniform, leaped into the air, and flew home at six hundred miles an hour.

I raced up three flights of stairs. I unlocked the door. I walked into my apartment.

"Mom? Dad? Tiffany?" I called. "Are you guys OK?"

No answer. In the kitchen was my mom with her back to me.

"Mom!" I shouted. I raced up to her. She was frozen stiff. Oh, no!

She couldn't be dead. She *couldn't*. Trying really hard not to cry, I held her wrist and took her pulse. I couldn't feel anything for a few seconds, and then . . . a beat! Just one, but a beat. That meant her heart was still pumping! That meant she was still alive! I kept holding her wrist, counting, waiting for another beat. When I got to sixty, I felt another beat.

Most healthy people's hearts beat sixty or seventy or eighty times a minute. Hers was beating *once* a minute. What the heck was going on here?

My dad was sitting at the kitchen table, reading a newspaper. I took his pulse. His pulse was the same as my mom's — one beat a minute.

I looked around for Tiffany, but I couldn't see her. Maybe she already left for school. The bathroom door was closed. I kicked it open. Tiffany was standing at the mirror with hot rollers in her hair. One of the rollers was dangling in front of her face. She looked so stupid, I felt sorry for her. I decided not to take her pulse. I mean, it was probably the same as my mom's and dad's anyway.

I couldn't understand why everybody was frozen, though.

Then I had a thought. I have this friend named Tortoise Man. He's a superhero like me, but he's an older guy, probably even older than my dad. He's pretty slow. He told me his top speed is five miles an hour. A really nice guy, though. Anyway, the only power he has is something he calls the Tortoise Ray. It slows things and people down to his speed. He used his ray to save us from a supervillain called the Tastemaker. Could Tortoise Man have something to do with all this? I had to find out.

Tortoise Man lives in an old VW microbus under a bridge in Washington, D.C. It was a nice clear day. Flying to Washington shouldn't take me more than twenty minutes, if I didn't smash into any planes or really big birds.

CHAPTER 2

There was no answer when I knocked on the door of Tortoise Man's microbus. The door wasn't locked, so I went inside.

Tortoise Man and Tortoise Woman, his wife, were in the front seat of the van. Playing Scrabble. Frozen stiff. I happen to be a pretty good Scrabble player. Even though I was here on emergency business, I couldn't help looking at the board. Tortoise Woman was winning. She'd gotten eighty-eight points with a Q word. Tortoise Man was in the middle of putting down a word when he got frozen: XZYBLRT. I hated to tell him, but XZYBLRT wasn't a word.

I didn't know what to do next. Should I fly over to the White House, which wasn't that far away, and check with the President? He was probably frozen, too. No, I had to think of what to do all by myself.

While I was thinking, I looked at the Scrabble board. I couldn't help taking a peek at the tiles Tortoise Man had. I realized I could make a word that would be worth ninety-one points, when I heard Tortoise Man move. I looked in his direction. He was blinking his eyes and shaking his head, like he'd just woken up.

"Tortoise Man, are you OK?" I asked.

"Whew!" he said. "Maximum Boy, what are *you* doing here?"

"There might be a national emergency," I said. "It looks like everybody in the whole country has been frozen stiff — even miniature schnauzers. How come you woke up?"

"I don't know," he said. "How long have I been out?"

I looked at my watch. It was nine-thirty.

"An hour," I said. "This started just as I got to school at eight-thirty."

"Oh," said Tortoise Man, "so tell me. Why'd you come here?"

"Well, I remembered your Tortoise Ray and how it slows things down. I thought maybe you had something to do with all this."

Tortoise Man got this really serious expression on his face.

"I can promise you, Maximum Boy," he said. "I had nothing at all to do with this."

Just then Tortoise Woman groaned and woke up.

"W-what happened?" she asked. "Oh, hello, Maximum Boy. Porter, did I fall asleep?"

"We both did, dear," said Tortoise Man. "Our young friend here tells me we're not the only ones. Apparently everybody in the country was frozen for an hour. So far we don't know why."

"Tell me, Tortoise Man," I said. "How does your Tortoise Ray work?"

"Well," said Tortoise Man, "all solid matter is made up of energy vibrating at a certain rate, right?"

"Right."

"So my Tortoise Ray beams out a signal

that drastically slows down the frequency at which everything is vibrating."

"I see."

"Obviously, dear," said Tortoise Woman, "somebody who knows the theory of your Tortoise Ray applied it. On a much larger scale."

"And," said Tortoise Man, "whoever did it could do it again."

"We must find whatever did this and destroy it," I said. "And put its inventor in jail."

Just then there was a knock on the door of the microbus. Tortoise Woman opened it. At the door stood somebody I recognized. Somebody I didn't much like.

"I'm Warren Blatt of the *International Enquirer*," he said. "I wondered if I could ask you a few questions."

"What are *you* doing here, Mr. Blatt?" I asked.

"I might ask you the same question, Maximum Boy," said Blatt. Then he turned to Tortoise Woman. "Can I come in, sis?"

"Of course," said Tortoise Woman.

Blatt climbed into the van. I thought it was rude for Blatt to call Tortoise Woman "sis." Unless she was his sister. Which I doubted.

"I'm asking you again, Mr. Blatt," I said. "What are you doing here?"

"Just doing my job, kid. The world stops, I want to know why. I got lots of questions. From what I hear, your pal here might have some of the answers."

"What do you mean?" said Tortoise Man.

"I mean the Tortoise Ray. I know all

about it. I know how it slows people down, just like what happened here. How about it, Tortoise Man? Is this your handiwork?"

"Of course not," said Tortoise Man. "Why would I want to do something like that?"

"I don't know, pal," said Blatt. "Maybe it had something to do with . . . your childhood?"

"What do you mean by that?"

"I mean I've done a little research on you, Tortoise Man. Or should I call you by your *real* name — Porter Torrington?"

Tortoise Woman gasped.

"How do you know that name?" she whispered.

"I know a lot of things, cookie," said Blatt. "I know that as a baby, Porter Torrington was stolen from his wealthy parents' home and left in the city aquarium by his absentminded kidnappers. . . ."

"W-where on earth did you . . . ?" gasped Tortoise Man.

"I know that he was found and brought up by a pair of kindly giant sea turtles. I know that he believed them to be his real

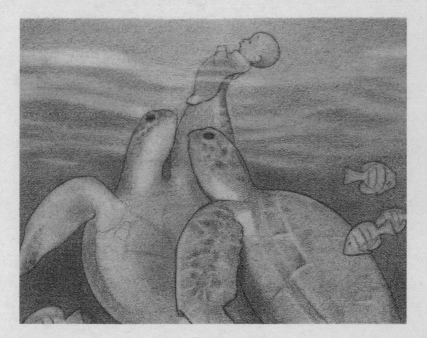

parents, and that he was twenty-one before finally learning the truth. . . ."

"This is outrageous!" said Tortoise Man. "These are lies, all lies!"

"Are they?" said Blatt. "I'll tell you what else I know. I know that Porter Torrington grew up as neither man nor turtle but somehow lacking the best qualities of both. I know that at age twenty-one he said goodbye to his amphibious foster parents and left the aquarium to get revenge on the fiends who kidnapped him so many years before."

"You can't prove any of this!" said Tortoise Woman.

"Oh, can't I?" said Blatt. "I can prove that and more. I can prove that Porter Torrington met and joined forces with karate master and marine biologist Sylvia Trundle.

I can prove that for years you were both feared by lawbreakers everywhere as Tortoise Man and Tortoise Woman. I can prove that you're both too tired and too slow now to scare anything but a nervous Chihuahua."

"You can prove nothing," said Tortoise Man.

"We'll see about that, pal," said Blatt. "The question is, why did you use the Tortoise Ray today to stop the world?"

"Mr. Blatt," said Tortoise Man, "I'm going to have to ask you to leave now."

"Fine," said Blatt. "I'll go. I'll be glad to go. But do you really think that kicking me out of your van is going to stop the world from learning the truth about you?"

"I don't know," said Tortoise Man, "but it's a start."

Blatt turned and looked at the Scrabble board.

"And for your information, pal," he said, "XZYBLRT isn't a word."

That was when my beeper went off. I looked at the number. It was the President calling me.

"Do you mind if I use your phone?" I asked. "It's a local call."

They nodded. I dialed. The President himself answered the phone.

"Max," said the President, "some fiend has managed to stop the world for an hour."

"I know, sir. Why would anybody do that? I mean, what good would it do them?"

"What good? I'll tell you what good," said the President. "I've just received word from the FBI. During the hour the world was stopped, four of the greatest treasures in the world were stolen."

"You're kidding me! What did they take, sir?"

"They stole the Hope Diamond, which was at New York's Museum of Natural History, on loan from the Smithsonian. From England's Tower of London they stole the Crown Jewels. From the Louvre museum in Paris they stole the most famous painting in the world — the Mona Lisa by Leonardo da Vinci. And from Fort Knox in Kentucky they stole a billion dollars in gold bullion."

"A billion in bullion!" I said.

"Yes," said the President. "Do you know what gold bullion is?"

"Sure. That's what my mom uses to make soup."

"No, Max, that's *beef* bouillon."

"Oh."

"Well, Max, that's the *bad* news. The *good* news is that all four places that were robbed had security cameras running. The videotapes will show us exactly who the robbers were."

"That's great, sir."

"As soon as we find out who the robbers are, I'll send you out to capture them."

"Uh, OK."

I was going to ask the President why he needed *me* to capture the robbers, why he couldn't just send the FBI or somebody to do that. But then I figured it might be rude to ask, so I just said good-bye and hung up the phone.

CHAPTER 3

By the time I got back to my parents' house in Chicago, it was almost ten-thirty.

"Max," said my mom, "what are you doing home? Why aren't you in school?"

"Mom, I've been to school and I've even been to Washington," I said. "I just came home to make sure you guys are all right."

"Oh, we're fine, dear. Why do you ask?"

"Well, the whole world stopped for an

hour. I was here earlier and found you and Dad and Tiffany frozen stiff."

"Oh, that," she said. "Yes, now that you mention it, we *were* frozen for a little while, but it didn't seem to have hurt us. So Tiffany went off to school, and your father is in his studio, painting." My dad's a really terrific artist and my mom teaches part-time. I don't know if I mentioned that.

"Mom, didn't you wonder why you got frozen?" I asked.

"Well, Daddy and I thought it might have been something we ate, so I threw out the orange juice. Sometimes it thaws during shipping. When the store employees re-freeze it, it can go bad. That's what we thought it was. Shouldn't you be in school, though, Max?"

"I guess so," I said.

*   *   *

"Max," said Mrs. Mulvahill, "you missed all the excitement."

"Oh, really?" I said. "What excitement was that, Mrs. Mulvahill?"

"When school began, everything stopped for a whole hour. Nothing moved. Then it started up again. Neither I nor anyone in class remembers a thing about it. Where were *you* when all that was going on?"

What I *wanted* to say was, I was right *here*, Mrs. Mulvahill. I saw you all frozen. I saw Ben frozen just as he was about to throw a ball of paper. I saw Jennifer frozen, just as she was painting her fingernail black. I saw Sherman frozen with his finger all the way up his nostril. But if I said that, I'd have to explain why *I* wasn't frozen for more than a few minutes, and where I went after that, and all the rest of it. I couldn't do that if I was going to keep my identity as Maximum Boy a secret.

"I, uh, overslept," I said.

"You overslept?" said Mrs. Mulvahill. "Well, that's too bad, Max. Because now I'm going to have to mark you late and give you detention."

It's tough being a superhero. Sometimes I wonder if it's all worth it.

CHAPTER 4

By the time I got out of detention, the late-afternoon editions of the newspapers were already on the street. The headlines on all the papers were about the stopping of the world: TREASURES STOLEN AS WORLD SLEPT! THIEVES' IDENTITY STILL UNKNOWN! said the *Chicago Tribune*. SECURITY CHIEF AT NATURAL HISTORY MUSEUM: YOU SNOOZE, YOU LOSE! said the *Chicago Sun-Times*.

When I got home, my dad was watching a story about it on TV.

The next day after school I was in the supermarket with my dad. At the checkout counter I saw a stack of new *International*

Enquirers. My dad and I love to look at the headlines on the *Enquirer*. They're so stupid, they make us laugh. I looked at the headline on today's *Enquirer*. It didn't make me laugh.

OVER-THE-HILL, WASHED-UP, FORMER SUPERHERO IS SUSPECT IN TREASURE THEFT! TORTOISE MAN ADMITS HIS RAY SLOWS THINGS DOWN!

Oh, no! It was Blatt's story. I speed-read it. It was worse than I thought. Blatt had done a real job on poor Tortoise Man. He'd deliberately misquoted and humiliated him. Tortoise Man was probably feeling awful about it. I thought I'd better go and try to cheer him up.

After a quick uniform change in the supermarket bathroom, I said good-bye to my dad, raced outside, and jumped into the air. It took me about twenty minutes of fast flying before I reached Washington.

"He's pretty depressed," said Tortoise Woman when she opened the door of the microbus. "I don't even know if he'll talk to you. Come on in, though."

I climbed into the microbus.

"Porter?" said Tortoise Woman. "Somebody here to see you."

"Who?" said a voice from the back of the microbus.

"A friend of yours from Chicago."

"I don't *have* any friends," said the voice.

"Tortoise Man," I said, "it's me, Maximum Boy. I need your help. I want you to help me find the madman who stopped the world and stole all those treasures."

"I can't help you, Maximum Boy. I can't help anybody. Didn't you read Blatt's article in the *Enquirer*? I'm over-the-hill, washed-up, and a complete loser. And, as of today, I'm giving up crime fighting forever."

"You're not over-the-hill or washed-up or a loser," I said. "You're terrific. Remember when we were captured by the Tastemaker? Your Tortoise Ray saved my life!"

"Blatt says my Tortoise Ray slowed the world down so I could steal all those treasures."

"Blatt's a jerk," I said.

Just then my beeper went off. I looked at the number. It was the President.

"Do you mind if I use your phone again?" I asked.

"Go right ahead, dear," said Tortoise Woman.

"Hello, Max," said the President. His voice sounded kind of grim.

"Is anything wrong, sir?" I asked. "You sound kind of grim."

"Max," said the President, "the security tapes have been analyzed. The robber has been identified."

"Really?" I said. "That's great! Who is it, sir?"

"I think you'd better come in and look at these tapes yourself."

"Can't you just tell me who the robber is?" I asked.

"No," said the President, "I'll show you when you get here."

I left Tortoise Man and Tortoise Woman. Five minutes later I was in the Oval Office.

"Hi there, Mr. President," I said.

"Sit down, Max," said the President.

He didn't shake my hand or ask how my family was or anything like that. He looked really serious. I sat down. He put a tape into his VCR and pushed a button.

"This is the tape from the Louvre art museum in Paris," he said.

The tape began. On a wall in front of the camera hung the famous Mona Lisa painting. People were standing and admiring it. Suddenly, everybody standing and admiring the painting froze. A moment later, someone raced in, grabbed the painting off the wall, and quickly carried it away. The thief was a boy. *The thief was wearing a black pinstriped baseball uniform, a silver cape, and a black baseball cap with the letters MB on it!*

CHAPTER 5

"Well, Max?" said the President.

"Sir, I don't understand this," I said. "I didn't steal that painting."

"No? I will now show you the next tape," said the President. "This one is from the Tower of London in England."

He put in the next tape. Two royal Beefeater guards, dressed in red uniforms and black hats, stood guarding a table. A lot of people were standing around, admiring what was on the table. The table was covered with a purple velvet cloth. On top of the purple velvet cloth was a glass case. A gold crown and a lot of diamonds and rubies and emeralds and stuff were inside the glass case. Suddenly, the people and the guards froze. Then a kid dressed in a black baseball uniform and a silver cape raced in, took the crown and the jewels out of the case, and raced off. The kid sure looked like me.

"Do you have anything to say *now*, Max?" asked the President.

"Sir, I did not steal the Crown Jewels," I said.

"Is that so?" said the President. "The next tape is from Fort Knox, Kentucky."

This tape showed a huge stack of gold bars. Soldiers with rifles marched back and forth in front of the stack of gold bars. Suddenly, the marching guards froze in midstep. A kid in a black baseball uniform and a silver cape rolled a wheelbarrow up to the stack of gold bars. Boy, did he ever look like me! He filled the wheelbarrow full of gold, then rolled it away.

"And what about now?" asked the President.

I shook my head.

"Sir, I did not steal the beef bouillon," I said.

"*Gold* bullion," said the President.

"Whatever. I did not steal it."

"Is that so?" said the President. He put in another tape. "The next tape is from the Museum of Natural History in New York," he said.

This tape was a lot like the one from the

Tower of London. A diamond the size of an egg was resting on a red velvet cloth inside a glass case. A guard in a dark blue uniform stood watching as a crowd of men, women, and children admired it. Then, just like on the other tapes, everybody froze. And in came a kid in a black baseball uniform and a silver cape, who grabbed the diamond out of the case and ran away. This time I got a really good look at the kid. He was wearing glasses and had braces exactly like mine.

"Well, Max?" said the President. "How do you explain these tapes?"

"I don't know, sir, but this is crazy," I said. "I wasn't anywhere *near* the Louvre in Paris when the world stopped. And I wasn't anywhere near the Tower of London, either. Or Fort Knox. Or the Museum of Natural

History in New York. I was in Chicago, sir, in school!"

"Max," said the President, "don't lie to me. I saw the same tapes you did. It's pretty clear to me who stole those treasures. And I wouldn't be at all surprised to learn your friend Tortoise Man helped you do it. I want you to go home now and think about what you did. Then I want you to come back and tell me what we should do with you."

CHAPTER 6

I was pretty upset. After all I'd done for the President, to have him accuse me of being a thief? I couldn't believe it. It was so unfair!

I needed to be with my family. I flew back to Chicago.

"Mom, Dad, Tiffany," I said, "I have something awful to tell you."

"My heavens," said my mom, "what is it, Max?"

"I've just come from Washington. The President thinks I'm the thief who stole the Hope Diamond, the Mona Lisa, the Crown Jewels, and the beef bouillon from Fort Knox."

"Don't you mean *gold* bullion?" asked my dad.

"Whatever," I said. "The point is, I didn't do it. I *couldn't* have done it. Even though I've seen security tapes with me on them. The President thinks I'm a thief. What does my family think?"

"Max," said my dad, "if you tell me you didn't steal those things, that's good enough for me."

"Me, too," said Mom. "The *nerve* of that

President for not believing you. Especially after all you've done for him. Bringing back the island of Manhattan, and stopping that man who made everything taste like broccoli, and I don't know what all. I'm not one bit sorry I didn't vote for him now. I might just call him up and give him a piece of my mind."

"Thanks, Mom," I said, "but I'm not sure that would be such a good idea."

I turned to my sister.

"What about you, Tiff? Do you think I'm a thief?"

"No way," said Tiffany.

"Good," I said.

"But if you *did* do it, Max," said Tiffany, "could I please keep the Hope Diamond in my room? Right on top of my dresser? Could I, please? It would be so cool. I would take real good care of it, and I wouldn't show it to anybody or tell anybody about it, I promise."

"Tiffany, I don't *have* the Hope Diamond. I didn't steal all that stuff."

"Max, you are so selfish!" cried Tiffany. "Mom, make Max give me the Hope Diamond! Make him! Please!"

"Tiffany, be quiet," said Dad.

"It's not fair!" said Tiffany. "If Max has got the Crown Jewels and the Mona Lisa and all that gold bullion, can't he just give me one measly old Hope Diamond? Is that asking so much?"

"Tiffany Silver," said my dad, "you go to your room this minute and stay there until you can control yourself!"

The next morning my dad went down to the newsstand early and bought lots of newspapers, including some out-of-town ones. The headlines were all about me.

This was the headline on the *Chicago Tribune*: SUPERHERO . . . OR SUPER THIEF? LOCAL HERO BECOMES NATIONAL DISGRACE! This was the headline on the *Chicago Sun-Times*: MAXIMUM BOY IS THIEF, NATION ROCKED BY NEWS! This was the headline on the *New York Post*: IS MAXBOY BURGLAR? PREZ SEZ YEZ! The story even made the newspapers in Europe. The headline on the biggest newspaper in Paris, *Le Monde*, said: MOXIMUM BOY EES ZE ROBBER!

I turned on the TV. The news there wasn't any better. They had an interview with the mayor of New York, who gave me the key to the city when I saved Manhattan. "I'd like to call upon Maximum Boy to return the Hope Diamond to New York," said the mayor. "I'd also like him to return the key to the city. And my wallet — it's been missing ever since I gave him that key to the city."

There was an interview with the governor of California, who erected a huge statue of me in the state capitol after I saved them from the Tastemaker. "We don't want a statue of an accused thief in California," said the governor. "Tomorrow the statue of Maximum Boy will be flown out of here by helicopter and used to plug a hole in Hoover Dam."

There were angry crowds outside the Tower of London. They carried signs that read: JAIL THE THIEF! GIVE MAXIMUM BOY THE MAXIMUM! There were angry crowds outside the Louvre in Paris. They carried signs that

read: JAIL ZE THIEF! GEEVE MOXIMUM BOY ZE
MOXIMUM! I was so hurt and angry I felt like
crying. Superheroes aren't technically supposed to cry.

While I was watching all this on TV, the
President called.

"Max, there are angry crowds outside the White House. They're shouting for your arrest."

"Yes, sir."

"Frankly, Max, they're embarrassing and distracting. I'm going to have to put an end to it."

"Good. You're going to tell them I'm innocent?"

"No, Max. I'm going to tell you to turn yourself in."

"Turn myself in?" I said. "To who?"

"The police."

"But, sir, I'm not guilty! I never stole all that stuff!"

"Max, please. Don't insult my intelligence. We've both seen the tapes."

"Look, sir," I said. "I'm only one person. How could I possibly be in New York, London, Paris, and Fort Knox at the same time?"

"The places weren't robbed at exactly the same time, Max. They were robbed about ten minutes apart. You can fly ten thousand miles an hour if you want to. You could have pulled off all four robberies easily."

My mom and dad finally decided that the best thing to do was hire a lawyer to defend me, then to turn myself in to the police.

CHAPTER 7

The lawyer my mom and dad hired to defend me was named Lester Boogerfinger. He came over to our apartment to meet me.

Lester Boogerfinger wasn't much taller than me and probably weighed about the same. He wore a pin-striped black suit and vest, a black shirt, a white tie, and sunglasses. He spoke in a high, squeaky voice.

He must have thought the black shirt and the sunglasses made him look tough. What it actually made him look like was a kid in a Halloween gangster costume.

"Well, young man," squeaked Lester Boogerfinger. "You sure got yourself in one heck of a mess, didn't you? You'll be lucky if they don't send you to the electric chair."

"What?" I said.

"Just kidding, Max, just kidding!" said Lester Boogerfinger. He slapped me on the back, almost knocking me over.

Lester Boogerfinger wasn't the first person I'd have chosen to defend me. I took my dad aside and whispered in his ear.

"Dad, can we get somebody else?" I whispered.

"What's wrong with Mr. Boogerfinger?" whispered my dad.

"Well, for one thing, that remark about sending me to the electric chair."

"He was kidding, Max, didn't you hear him say that?"

"And for another thing," I said, "there's his name. I don't think anybody is going to take me seriously with a lawyer named Boogerfinger."

"Max," said Dad, "we mustn't make fun of people just because they have stupid or disgusting names. It isn't fair."

"I know," I said. "But isn't there any other lawyer we could get?"

"Well," said Dad, "I did hear about another lawyer who's supposed to be pretty good. His name is Morton Smellybottom. Do you want me to give him a call?"

"Never mind," I said. "I'll stick with Boogerfinger."

Mom and Dad wanted to go with me to the police station when I turned myself in, but I said no. If they did, everybody would find out my true identity, and then my family would be in danger. So, wearing my Maximum Boy uniform, I walked into the Grant Park Police Station with Lester Boogerfinger.

Three policemen were standing around, talking and laughing. They didn't even see us come in. On a high platform stood a desk. Behind the desk sat the desk sergeant, reading a comic book.

It was scary to turn myself in. I'd never been arrested before. I've never been in jail before. I didn't know what to expect. I didn't know what to do. I thought Lester Boogerfinger ought to announce who I was, or introduce me or something. I looked at him for help. He shrugged.

He obviously didn't know what to do, any more than I did. I walked up to the desk. I took a deep breath.

"Excuse me," I said in a loud, clear voice. "I'm Maximum Boy and I'm here to turn myself in." I pointed to Lester Boogerfinger. "This is my lawyer, Mr. Boogerfinger."

The desk sergeant looked up from his comic book. He frowned and looked at me blankly.

"Excuse me," said the desk sergeant. "I didn't hear you because I was reading a very important document. Now who is this Mr. Snotfinger?"

"Not *Snot*finger, *Booger*finger," squeaked Lester Boogerfinger. "I'm this boy's attorney."

"Thank you, Mr. Mucusfinger," said the desk sergeant. He turned back to me. "And who'd you say *you* were?"

The cops who'd been talking stopped and stared at me.

"Maximum Boy?" I repeated. "The person who's supposed to have stolen the Hope Diamond, the Crown Jewels, the Mona Lisa, and the gold from Fort Knox? I'm here to turn myself in."

The instant I said that, the three cops whipped out their pistols. They dropped into a two-handed firing crouch, their guns pointed right in my face.

"Freeze, Maximum Boy!" shouted one of the cops. "You're under arrest!"

The desk sergeant picked up his phone. "We've just captured Maximum Boy!" he said. "Get the media down here immediately!"

"But, sir," I said, "I came here of my own free will. I came here to give myself up."

"Grab him, men!" shouted the desk sergeant. "Cuff him!"

A second cop roughly grabbed my wrists and snapped on handcuffs.

"You have the right to remain silent," he said. "You have the right to an attorney . . ."

"I thought you'd *appreciate* my turning myself in," I said. "I thought you'd at least treat me politely."

". . . If you choose not to remain silent," continued the cop who had cuffed me, "anything you say can and will be used against you in a court of law . . ."

"Why are you handcuffing me?" I asked. "I'm Maximum Boy. You know I could break out of these cuffs in a second if I wanted to."

"You hear that, men?" shouted the desk sergeant. "He's going to break out of his cuffs! He's going to try to escape!"

"I'm not trying to escape!" I yelled. "If I was trying to escape, why would I walk in here and give myself up?"

I turned to Lester Boogerfinger for help. He was watching all this as if it were a really interesting program on TV.

"Mr. Boogerfinger!" I called out. "Can't you help me out here?"

"Of course," said Lester Boogerfinger in his high squeaky voice. "Officers, my client is not trying to escape. Max is a nice boy who'd never do anything as rude as escape!"

Max? He called me Max! Was he about to blow my secret identity, too?

"*Pssstt!*" I said to Lester Boogerfinger and shook my head.

He realized what he'd done and smacked his forehead.

"When I called my client *Max*," said

Lester Boogerfinger, "that was because 'Max' is short for 'Maximum Boy.' It is *not* because his real name is Max, because it isn't. His real name is actually . . . *Melvin*."

"Melvin? Melvin what?" said the desk sergeant.

"Melvin . . . Sssssssilver . . ." said Lester Boogerfinger.

"Melvin *Silver*?" said the desk sergeant.

"No! Melvin . . . Silver . . . service . . ." said Lester Boogerfinger. "Yes, that's it, Melvin Silverservice."

"Well, then," said the desk sergeant, "please tell Mr. Silverservice not to try to escape, Mr. Nostriljuice."

"My name isn't *Nostriljuice*, it's *Boogerfinger*!" screamed Lester Boogerfinger. "B-O-O-G-E-R-F-I-N-G-E-R!"

The door of the police station opened

and in came the media. Reporters from all the networks and cable TV. Reporters from the *Chicago Tribune* and the *Chicago Sun-Times*. They rushed toward me with note-pads, microphones, and TV lights.

"Maximum Boy!" shouted a reporter. "What turned you from superhero to super thief?"

"Maximum Boy has no comment!" squeaked Lester Boogerfinger.

"Yes, I have!" I said. "My comment is that I'm not a thief. I didn't steal those things."

"Then why are you turning yourself in?" asked another reporter.

"Because my picture seems to be on the security tapes."

"How could you not be the thief if you're on the security tapes?"

"I don't know," I said. "Look, in court you're innocent until proven guilty, right?"

"Yes, but in the news you're guilty until proven innocent," said another reporter.

The cops took me to a cell and locked me inside. Lester Boogerfinger stood outside my cell, looking serious.

"What's going to happen to me now, Mr. Boogerfinger?"

"Don't worry, Max," he said. "I've got a plan."

"Good. What's your plan?"

"You're going to plead guilty," he said. "It's fast and it's cheap. And I'll try to get you a light sentence."

"A light sentence? How light?"

"I think I might be able to get you only seventeen years."

"Seventeen *years*? Look, Mr. Boogerfinger, I'm not pleading guilty — I'm innocent!"

"Max, get serious. You're on the security tapes. How could you possibly be innocent?"

"So you think I'm guilty, too? My own lawyer thinks I'm guilty?"

"It doesn't matter what *I* think, Max," he said. "It only matters what the jury thinks."

"Have you ever defended somebody you thought was guilty?" I asked.

"No. But I've never defended anybody I thought was innocent, either."

"What kind of defense attorney are you if you've never defended anybody who was guilty or innocent?"

"Who said I'm a defense attorney? I'm a *patent* attorney."

"What's a patent attorney?"

"If you invent something and you don't

want anybody to steal your idea, a patent attorney helps you get a patent on it to protect it. Which reminds me. If you have any inventions you'd like to patent, this might be a dandy time to talk about them."

CHAPTER 8

When Lester Boogerfinger left, I got really depressed. How the heck could I prove I was innocent if my own lawyer thought I was guilty? And how the heck could I prove I was innocent if I was in jail? Come to think of it, if I was in jail, how could I keep up with my schoolwork?

About an hour after Boogerfinger left, a cop came to my cell.

"There's a phone call for you, kid," said the cop. "You want to take it?"

"Who's it from?"

"Somebody named Noodleman."

Noodleman from the League of Super-heroes! Noodleman could stretch himself into a very long, very thin piece of pasta and hide out in bowls of spaghetti and linguine to spy on bad guys. He was nowhere near as famous as Superman or Batman or Wonder Woman, but he was definitely a superhero. And if he was calling me, it meant that my fellow superheroes were going to come to my rescue!

The cop opened my cell. He escorted me down the hallway to a phone mounted on the brick wall.

"Hi, Noodleman, it's Maximum Boy," I said happily.

"Maximum Boy, the League of Super-heroes has heard about your situation, and . . ."

"And . . . ?"

"And I'm calling to let you know officially that the League of Superheroes is shocked that you could have done such a thing."

"What?" I said. I couldn't believe my ears.

"You are a disgrace to your uniform, Maximum Boy. As of today, you are officially expelled from the League of Super-heroes."

There was a click on the other end of the line.

I couldn't believe it. I just couldn't believe it. Deserted first by the President of the United States, and then by my fellow superheroes! It was so unfair. It was just too much. I burst into tears.

"Crybaby!" said the cop disgustedly. "Teensy-weensy wittow babesy. OK, Mr. Crybaby, back to your cell before I have to change your teensy-weensy wittow diaper."

That cop made me so mad, I stopped crying. When I was back in my cell, I gave myself a little pep talk. *Hey, Maximum Boy*, I said, *cut the tears. Remember who you are. You're a kid who punches out supervillains. You're a kid who picks up eighteen-wheeler tractor trailers with one hand. You're a kid who flies faster than a Stealth bomber. If you wanted to, you could stick your arm down that cop's throat and pull him inside out like a sock.*

Right away I felt better. I knew if I wanted to I could bend back the bars of this

cell and walk right out of here, and no cops could stop me, either. The only problem was, I was supposed to *uphold* the law, not break it.

On the other hand, I didn't want to miss dinner at my house. We were having pepperoni pizza tonight — my favorite.

So this is what I decided to do. As soon as the cop was gone, I turned myself into a human drill. I stood up straight and tall and wrapped my arms around my body and started spinning. I spun faster and faster till my feet made a hole in the floor of the cell. I burrowed my way straight through the floor. Then I burrowed underground for about a block and came out through a sewer. Then, promising myself I'd burrow back into my cell before morning, I flew home.

"Max!" said my mother. "Don't tell me

you're home already! I was just about to serve dinner."

"Did Mr. Boogerfinger get you out of jail?" asked my dad.

"Not exactly," I said.

"Then how did you get them to let you out?"

"It's a long story, Dad," I said. "And I have to go back there right after dinner. So could we just eat?"

"Pee-yew!" said Tiffany. "You smell like a sewer! Where have you been?"

"In a sewer," I said.

As soon as dinner was over, I speed-washed the dishes before my stupid sister, Tiffany, could complain I wasn't doing my share of the chores. Then I flew off to Washington.

On the way I had a terrible thought:

What if it really was *me on the tapes? After all, I did black out for a short time right after I got to school. What if I really* had *committed all four robberies during that time, then got amnesia, and forgot? What then?*

I couldn't afford to think about that now. What I had to do now was find whatever it was that stopped the world. If I could do that, then I'd find the person who built it and stole the treasures. And that person could explain why I was on all of the security tapes. Maybe it wasn't me after all. Maybe it was just somebody *dressed* like me. *Four* somebodies dressed like me.

Well, whatever the explanation was, I couldn't do this alone. I really needed the help of Tortoise Man. And last I heard, Tortoise Man had given up crime fighting forever.

CHAPTER 9

"Hi, Maximum Boy," said Tortoise Woman. "If you're here to see Porter, I'm afraid you've made the trip for nothing."

"He's still depressed?"

"In his *best* moods he's depressed. And right now he's not in one of his best moods. Say, I heard you were in jail in Chicago."

"Well, technically, I am. But I really need to talk to him. Is he here?"

"I'll check. Porter? Are you here? Maximum Boy has come all the way from a Chicago jail to talk to you."

"How could you not know if I'm here?" asked Tortoise Man in a grouchy voice. "This isn't a forty-room house, it's a stinking *microbus*."

"Oh, hi there, Tortoise Man," I said. "I came to ask your help. I need you to help me find the machine that stopped the world and the fiend who invented it."

"Then what you need is a superhero," said Tortoise Man. "Try the Yellow Pages under Superheroes. I'm no superhero. I'm an over-the-hill, washed-up, middle-aged loser. If you don't believe me, read the *International Enquirer*. Now go away, kid. I've still got three hours of sulking to do before bedtime and I'm way behind."

"If you're going to believe everything you read in the newspapers," I said, "then I'm the thief who stole all those treasures."

"Well, I hope you're enjoying them," grumbled Tortoise Man.

I took out the business card Tortoise Man had given me when I first met him.

"Look what it says on your business card," I said. TORTOISE MAN: SUPERHERO, CHAMPION OF THE WEAK, ENEMY OF EVILDOERS EVERYWHERE, HANDYMAN, NO JOB TOO BIG OR TOO SMALL.

"Go away, Maximum Boy. The *International Enquirer* was right. I'm not cut out for the justice racket after all. I'm a failure as a superhero. Tortoise Man is turning in his shell."

"Porter," said Tortoise Woman, "if you give up now, what will happen to the cause of liberty and justice in this land we call America?"

"I don't know the answer to that, Sylvia," said Tortoise Man. "I don't know the answer to a *lot* of things. Heck, I don't even know what I'm doing anymore."

"Neither do I," said Tortoise Woman. "Neither do a lot of people. Reporters like Warren Blatt don't know what *they're* doing, but it doesn't stop *them*, does it?"

"You do have a point there," said Tortoise Man.

"Porter," said Tortoise Woman, "you can't give up your whole career in crime fighting just because you've lost one demeaning, degrading, humiliating battle after another! You just can't!"

Tortoise Man sighed.

"I guess you're right," he said. "OK,

Maximum Boy. If you really want me, I'm back on board. Where do we start?"

"We start by figuring out who's the fiend who stopped the world and stole the treasures," I said.

"It would have to be someone evil enough to plan such a thing," said Tortoise Woman. "Someone who knows you well enough to figure out how the Tortoise Ray works."

"Hmmm," said Tortoise Man.

"Someone brilliant enough to create such a machine," I said. "Someone who's as interested as you in slowing things down."

Tortoise Man snapped his fingers.

"I know of only one man who fits that description," he said. "Ethelred the Unready. We were roommates in college."

"Ethelred the Unready!" said Tortoise Woman. "Of course!"

"Who the heck is Ethelred the Unready?" I asked.

"A brilliant villain whose evil deeds would be world-famous today," said Tortoise Woman, "except that he takes so long leaving the house, he never has time to do them properly."

"And you actually roomed with this guy in college?" I asked. "What was he like?"

"Not a bad fellow," said Tortoise Man. "Would've been an even better fellow if he'd changed his underwear more than once a month, but not a bad fellow. Majored in electrical engineering and music, with a minor in robbery. Could have been a brilliant engineer or a concert violinist, but he never got his homework in on time. And he was late to every exam. So instead of graduating college, he was forced into a life of crime."

"Even in *crime* his lateness was a problem," said Tortoise Woman. "Ethelred would get to a bank for a robbery at least ten minutes late — ten minutes after the week's cash had been taken away by an armored truck. Whatever he did, he was always at least ten minutes late."

"In school," said Tortoise Man, "he tried to fool himself. Set his watch ten minutes fast so he'd be on time. That never worked. He always knew it was ten minutes fast. It makes perfect sense that Ethelred would build a slow-motion machine. To slow everyone else down so he could be on time."

"But with the slow-motion machine, he made sure he had enough time," I said. "With the slow-motion machine, he managed to get away with four of the world's greatest treasures."

"True," said Tortoise Man.

"Do you know where Ethelred the Unready hangs out now?" I asked.

Tortoise Woman took a small, scruffy-looking phone book out of the glove compartment and started riffling through it. "Hmmm," said Tortoise Woman. "The *Directory of Archvillains and Evildoers* lists a secret mountain hideout in the hills above Sheboygan, Wisconsin."

"I know that area," I said. "My parents used to take me and my sister there for summer vacations. Tortoise Man, let's go there immediately."

"How would we get there?"

"We'll fly," I said. "I'll carry you."

"Can you carry somebody as big as me? I'm kind of overweight."

"Tortoise Man, I've carried armored trucks to the South Pole."

"Well, I don't know what good I'll be to you," said Tortoise Man. "I'm washed-up and over-the-hill. But I'll come along for the ride, if you like."

We took off immediately. I carried Tortoise Man, clutching his shell with both hands.

It was very dark and very cold, flying through the air at seven hundred miles an hour. It was also very beautiful. Below us were the lit-up buildings of the capital — the Supreme Court, the White House, the Washington Monument, and all the rest. I'd

seen them lots of times before from this height, but I never got tired of the sight.

We headed north and west. We passed over the westernmost tip of Maryland, then Pennsylvania, the upper tip of Ohio, Lake Erie, and the state of Michigan. Below us were woodsy areas that were completely black. Then came clusters of tiny lights that were small villages. They looked like Christmas tree lights. Just past Lake Michigan was Wisconsin. By the time we got to Lake Michigan the clouds grew thick and the winds were brutal. We were blown up and down and all over the place.

"You OK, Tortoise Man?" I yelled above the shrieking of the wind.

"I'm good!" he shouted.

"Well, fasten your seat belt!" I called. "We're encountering a little turbulence!"

Just then there was an amazing flash of blue-white lightning, followed by an explosion of thunder so loud I nearly wet my pants. I don't know if you've ever been up in an airplane during an electrical storm. Well, it's about eighty times scarier *without* the plane.

We couldn't see the ground at all now. The wind tossed us around so much, I completely lost my sense of direction. I decided to fly closer to the ground. Maybe I could get below the clouds and find something I recognized. Coming down through the clouds, I spotted what looked like an old stone castle, sitting on a mountaintop.

"That's it!" Tortoise Man shouted. "That's Ethelred's hideout!"

CHAPTER 10

I landed on a rocky ledge just outside the castle. Turrets about thirty feet high rose from the top of the castle. Built into one of the turrets was a clock tower with a tremendous clock at the top. A huge radio antenna stood on the castle's highest turret. That antenna could be part of the slow-motion transmitter that stopped the world.

Next to the castle stood a small, two-

seater helicopter. Sheets of rain hit us side-
ways in the face. We couldn't have been
wetter. Rivers of water were running under-
neath my uniform.

"Have you been here before?" I asked.

"No, but I've seen pictures," said Tortoise Man.

There was another flash of lightning
and another explosion of thunder. My throat
was getting sore. Mom was going to make
me gargle with salt water the minute I got
home.

Tortoise Man led the way to a side en-
trance of the castle. Inside, the lights were
on. Somebody was definitely home. I yanked
the lock out of the door and opened it. We
crept inside.

The room we'd entered was dimly lit,
but I could see once my eyes got accustomed

to the light. The walls were made of rough stone. The room was filled with the sounds of ticking and bonging. Clocks of all shapes and sizes hung on the stone walls. Cuckoo clocks. Clocks with pendulums. Clocks that showed the time in every time zone of the country. In every time zone of the world. I checked my watch.

"Those clocks are all ten minutes fast," I whispered to Tortoise Man.

He chuckled. "That's my old friend Ethelred," he said.

Built into the stone wall was an enormous stainless-steel control panel with several digital clocks. All the digital clocks were set ten minutes fast. There were many buttons on the control panel, but three of them caught my attention. One read, SLOW, one read, PAUSE, and one read, RESET.

"This is it," I whispered. "The slow-motion machine!"

Tortoise Man nodded. "Yes," he said. "Or else it's just a fancy VCR."

Then I noticed something else on another wall. A big painting of a lady sitting in a chair.

"*Pssst*, Tortoise Man," I whispered. "Is this what I think it is?"

He looked at it and whistled.

"The Mona Lisa," he said. "The most famous painting in the world."

"I guess we've got the right castle," I said. "And I guess this digital machine isn't a fancy VCR."

At the end of the room a spiral staircase went way up into the clock tower about thirty feet above our heads. We heard something. People talking. We crept closer to the spiral staircase and peeked upward.

At the top of the tower, fooling with wheels and gears, was a guy about my dad's age. He had on a red uniform with clocks all over it. There was a big, round clock face on his back with a huge E in the middle. Just below him on the spiral staircase stood an old guy with white hair. The guy in the clock uniform was pretending not to listen to the old guy.

"The guy in the clock uniform is Ethelred the Unready," whispered Tortoise Man. "The guy below him is his servant, Wolfgang."

"On my signal," I whispered, "we jump them. You take Wolfgang, I'll fly up there and take Ethelred."

"Right," said Tortoise Man. "Listen, what if Wolfgang is stronger than I am?"

"Wolfgang is around eighty years old," I whispered. "You can take him."

"What if Wolfgang is a really *strong* eighty-year-old?"

"Tortoise Man," I whispered, "you're a superhero. You can do it."

It was a little hard to hear what Wolfgang was saying, above the storm outside. I crept closer to the spiral staircase and tried to listen.

"I *told* you there wouldn't be time to plant the dynamite and blow the door of that bank safe unless we left the hideout at exactly six o'clock," said Wolfgang. "Didn't I tell you that?"

Ethelred didn't answer.

"I warned you and I warned you, and you simply didn't listen to me," said Wolfgang. "And so what happened, Ethelred? Tell me. Did we have time to plant the dynamite or didn't we?"

Ethelred sighed a really big sigh.

"Did we have time to plant the dynamite or didn't we?" Wolfgang repeated.

"We *didn't* have time, Wolfgang. We *didn't* have time, all right?"

"And what did we learn from this experience, Ethelred? Did it teach us to leave the hideout on time or didn't it?"

"Probably not," said Ethelred.

"I didn't think so," said Wolfgang.

"*Now*," I whispered.

Tortoise Man and I bounded into the clock tower. Tortoise Man grabbed Wolfgang by the ankles and pulled hard. Wolfgang screamed and crashed to the floor. I flew up the staircase and grabbed Ethelred.

"You're busted, Ethelred!" I said.

"I don't believe we've met," said Ethelred.

"Maximum Boy's my name and justice is my game," I said. The minute I said that I realized how boony it sounded.

"Ah, yes, Maximum Boy," said Ethelred. "The international super thief."

"If I'm the thief, then why's the Mona Lisa in your clock room?"

"The Mona Lisa? Sorry, the name doesn't ring a bell."

I yanked Ethelred down the staircase and shoved his face into the Mona Lisa.

"Perhaps *this* will refresh your memory," I said.

"What the . . . ? How did *that* get there?" he said.

Tortoise Man and Wolfgang were wrestling on the floor. Tortoise Man was pulling Wolfgang's hair. Wolfgang had his foot caught in Tortoise Man's shell. I couldn't tell who was winning, Tortoise Man or the eighty-year-old.

"OK, Ethelred," I said. "You want to tell me how you managed to steal four of the world's greatest treasures and make it look like I was the thief?"

"No," said Ethelred, "I want *you* to tell *me*."

"Fine," I said. "You find four kids about my age who don't mind breaking the law. You have four Maximum Boy uniforms made for them. The day of the robbery you fly one to New York, one to London, one to Paris, and one to Fort Knox. Each kid is fitted with a special device to neutralize the slow-motion frequency. At eight twenty-nine A.M. Central Standard Time, you program your slow-motion machine to slow the world down to a sixtieth of its regular speed. Each kid goes in and steals a treasure in front of the security cameras. Your henchmen are standing by off-camera to cart the treasures back to you. You get all the treasures, and I get blamed for all the thefts."

"You've got it all figured out, haven't you, Maximum Boy?"

"Pretty much," I said. "And there's no way I could have committed four robberies in four different cities at the same exact moment."

"The robberies didn't all start at the same exact moment," said Ethelred. "They started ten minutes apart."

"That was because you wanted to make it look like I robbed one place, then flew to another city and robbed the next place," I said.

"But if the first robbery started at eight twenty-nine Central Standard Time," said Ethelred, "then each of the four boys had to begin his theft ten minutes after the previous boy's. ALLOWING FOR THE CHANGES IN TIME ZONE FROM FORT KNOX TO NEW YORK TO LONDON TO PARIS, PLEASE CALCULATE WHAT TIME EACH LOCATION WAS ROBBED."

The room started to spin. Oh, no!

Ethelred had slipped me a math problem before I knew what was happening! I sank to my knees, weak and nauseous.

Aaaaarrgh!

"Quick, Wolfgang!" shouted Ethelred. "Get the chopper!"

I got woozy and all the strength left my body. Next to me I could dimly see Wolfgang break free of Tortoise Man and run for the door. Wolfgang was slow, but Tortoise Man was slower. Wolfgang was out the door and into the helicopter before Tortoise Man got halfway across the room.

"Porter, old man," said Ethelred to Tortoise Man. "So lovely to see you again."

He kicked Tortoise Man hard in the shell. Tortoise Man went down.

From outside I could hear that Wolfgang had the rotors going on the helicopter. Ethelred raced up the spiral staircase of the clock tower. He opened the window at the top and leaned out.

I dragged myself to the door and crawled outside. The rain was still coming down hard. Hard enough to start me sneezing and make my nose run. The helicopter had risen over the castle. It was hovering ten feet above the clock tower. Wolfgang dropped a rope ladder from the chopper. Ethelred crawled out the window of the clock tower and grabbed onto one of the huge iron hands on the face of the clock. The wind and rain whipped at his red clock uniform.

"Grab the ladder, Ethelred!" shouted Wolfgang from the helicopter.

Ethelred hesitated. If he missed, he'd fall off the clock tower.

The helicopter bucked and shuddered in the storm.

"Grab the ladder, Ethelred!" screamed Wolfgang. "I can't hold the chopper in place much longer!"

Ethelred looked at the rocky ground thirty feet below him. And at the edge of the cliff just beyond. He looked up at the ladder dangling from the chopper, just out of his reach.

"Grab it now!" shrieked Wolfgang.

Ethelred the Unready reached out for the ladder too late, just as the chopper was blown upward by the wind. He lost his grip on the clock hand and fell. He hit the ground and rolled to the edge of the cliff. He grabbed a bush, but he couldn't hold on. He slid over the edge and disappeared.

The chopper dove and tried to follow Ethelred down into the canyon. Then it pulled up sharply and disappeared in the storm.

CHAPTER 11

The President decided to hold a press lunch outside the White House in the Rose Garden. All the media were there — the networks, cable TV, all the local TV stations, reporters from newspapers and TV stations all over the world. The President seated me just to his right. He said it was the seat of honor.

Tortoise Man was seated on *my* right.

And my parents and Tiffany were in the audience, only they had to pretend they didn't know me.

Just before the President spoke to the press, guys in white jackets served us our lunch. It was linguine with clam sauce, which is kind of like spaghetti.

"Ladies and gentlemen of the press," said the President. "We are gathered here today to honor a very brave young man. A young man who has put his life on the line many times for our country. A young man who has, unfortunately, been misjudged and blamed by some for crimes he did not commit."

I liked everything he said up to the "blamed by *some*" part. I mean, the person who blamed me the most was the President himself!

"I have recommended to the Congress of

the United States that we honor this young man," said the President. "Therefore, at this time I present Maximum Boy with . . . the Congressional Medal of Honor."

Everybody broke into loud applause. The President slipped a big bronze medal on a blue-and-white ribbon around my neck. Then he shook hands with me.

Flashguns were going off on all sides of me. I had little green burn-out spots in front of my eyes.

"*Psssstt,*" said a tiny voice very close by. "Maximum Boy!"

I looked around. I couldn't tell who was calling me.

"Who's calling me?" I asked. "Where are you?"

"Down here," said the voice. "In the linguine."

I looked down at my bowl of linguine. One of the strands of linguine had a tiny head on it, and it was speaking to me.

"Hi, Maximum Boy. It's me, Noodleman."

"Noodleman," I said. "What are you doing here?"

"I came here to apologize to you. Unofficially, that is."

"The League of Superheroes sent you to apologize to me?" I asked.

"Yes. Unofficially, though. The League of Superheroes never apologizes officially."

"Why not?"

"They feel it would hurt their image. They feel apologies are . . . wimpy."

So that's pretty much what happened.

After the press lunch, the President

sent me, my mom and dad, and my sister, Tiffany, back to Chicago on *Air Force One*. I was glad to get home. Little did I know that the President would have a new assignment for me before the week was out. An assignment involving invaders from outer space!